P9-DFK-768

THERE'S SOMETHING IN MY ATTIC

written and illustrated by MERCER MAYER

A Puffin Pied Piper

BURNETT CHILDREN'S CENTER

PUFFIN PIED PIPER BOOKS
Published by the Penguin Group
Penguin Books USA Inc., 375 Hudson Street, New York, New York 10014, U.S.A.
Penguin Books Ltd, 27 Wrights Lane, London W8 5TZ, England
Penguin Books Australia Ltd, Ringwood, Victoria, Australia
Penguin Books Canada Ltd, 10 Alcorn Avenue, Toronto, Ontario, Canada M4V 3B2
Penguin Books (N.Z.) Ltd, 182-190 Wairau Road, Auckland 10, New Zealand
Penguin Books Ltd, Registered Offices: Harmondsworth, Middlesex, England

Originally published in hardcover by
Dial Books for Young Readers
A Division of Penguin Books USA Inc.

Copyright © 1988 by Mercer Mayer
All rights reserved
Library of Congress Catalog Card Number: 86-32875
Printed in the U.S.A.
First Puffin Pied Piper Printing 1992
ISBN 0-14-054813-0
9   10

A Pied Piper Book is a registered trademark of
Dial Books for Young Readers,
a division of Penguin Books USA Inc.,
® TM 1,163,686 and ® TM 1,054,312.

THERE'S SOMETHING IN MY ATTIC
is also available in hardcover from
Dial Books for Young Readers.

*The art for each picture consists of pen, ink, and watercolor
washes that are color-separated and reproduced in full color.*

To Jessie, my daughter,
with love

Who was touched by Goopy
and went to Singapore?
Who had witches in the trees
and a finger on the door?
Who didn't like the thumber
or the lightning anymore?

BURNETT CHILDREN'S CENTER

I was never afraid of anything
when we lived in the city,
but now we live on a farm.

At night when the lights go out,
I get scared,

because I can hear

a nightmare in the attic

right above my head.

It doesn't seem to bother Mom and Dad.

They say it's probably mice.

But it sounds too big to be mice.

I decided to lasso that nightmare
and bring it down to show them.

I'd just be brave and sneak quietly
into the attic with my lasso ready.

BURNETT CHILDREN'S CENTER
1520 OAKDALE AVENUE
SAN NCISCO. CA   VIA 94124

BURNETT CHILDREN'S CENTER

It wasn't there.
But I noticed a bunch of toys
I thought were lost
lying in a pile behind some boxes.

Something weird was going on for sure.
Then I heard it creeping up the stairs.

"Hey," I called. "That's my teddy bear! Give it to me!"
But the nightmare tried to sneak back down the stairs.

So I chased it.

Then I lassoed it.
It was hugging my bear as hard as it could.

BURNETT CHILDREN'S CENTER

"Be careful, Nightmare," I said,
"or you'll rip my bear."

I tried to get my bear back,
but it wouldn't let go.

So I pulled it down the hall
to my parents' room.

I flipped on the lights

to show them the nightmare I captured.
I was sure they would be amazed.

But nightmares are very tricky, and
sometimes they just slip away.

I'll just have to get my bear back tomorrow.